# Imogen
## and the Ark

## William Mayne

## Illustrated by Nick Maland

Hodder
Children's
Books

a division of Hodder Headline

*For Emma*

*to share*

*with Kathryn*

Text Copyright © 1999 William Mayne
Illustrations Copyright ©1999 Nick Maland

First published in Great Britain in 1999
by Hodder Children's Books

The right of William Mayne to be identified as the Author of the Work has been asserted by him
in accordance with the Copyright, Designs and Patents Act 1988.

10   9   8   7   6   5   4   3   2   1

A Catalogue record for this book is available from the British Library

ISBN 0340 74372 7

Printed and bound in Great Britain by
Clays Ltd, St Ives plc

Hodder Children's Books
A Division of Hodder Headline
338 Euston Road
London NW1 3BH

# ONE

Imogen and Grandpa walked along the river, past the shops, through the park, and into the country. They saw the fishing boats coming back. They heard seagulls shouting over scraps from them. The fishing boats went past, and there was just the river.

"It's a long river," said Imogen, when there were no more boats to be seen or heard. "And it's stopped happening." Without the boats not very much was going on. But Grandpa was walking to the sea.

"Look, Imogen," he said. "In the river." There was a clever-looking bird paddling just off the edge, staring down into the water. Imogen thought he was reading the river, like a newspaper. He put down his head suddenly. Imogen thought he had lost his glasses, but it wasn't that. He had caught a fish. When he swallowed it whole, it wriggled inside his neck.  Imogen remembered about teatime. That's how milk goes down, she thought.

But tea was a long way off. Grandpa was still walking to the sea. Imogen went with him, and forgot to look at things.

"Now," said Grandpa, standing still at last, "we have come right to the very end of the river."

The river had gone. It had run into the sea, and Imogen's eyes could not find the other side, because there was nothing to look at, no other side, just nowhere for ever.

"People used to go round the world from here," said Grandpa. "Or round the bay and home for tea."

"That was a good idea," said Imogen, thinking of teatime again. "But it's just as far back as round the world."

It was a long way back. One more fishing boat came up the river, so Imogen waved at it. It did not stop to give them a ride, or even wave.

"They might be pirates," said Grandpa. "All sorts of people sail round the world."

Seagulls came down to the pirates'

boat. Imogen walked the long way back to the park, and had two swings on the swing, for exercise. They came to the town, and there were shops to look at.

"I could just get a pencil," said Imogen, because there was a pencil shop.

"Or a scrubbing-brush," she said, because there was a scrubbing-brush shop.

She had some money with her, in case things had to be bought.

Grandpa took her across the road before the bicycle shop. "I just wanted to stroke them," she said. But she wanted a pet bicycle too, that would not let her fall off.

"Not today," said Grandpa.

Then there was the toyshop.

"I think we've come the wrong way," said Grandpa. "We'll be late for tea."

"We can go in," said Imogen. "The door is open."

"Only for a moment," said Grandpa. "I don't think we're allowed to buy anything. Granny does the shopping, not us."

Grandpa looked at trains. Imogen looked at dolls and dolls' clothes and furniture and cars. They were all much more than her money could buy.

I would like to buy something, she thought. A little thing that doesn't cost much.

"Granny does the shopping," said Grandpa. "Imogen, it's time we went home."

Imogen did not reply. She had not seen a little thing. She had seen the biggest thing in the shop, and it wasn't even new. She did not mind the paint of the boat part being chipped, she did not care that some of the roof was nearly

worn away, or that the house windows
had broken glass, or that the two lions
had only three legs each. She only knew
that she wanted them.

She wanted the whole Ark, and
what was in it. She wanted it all, just as
it was. She stood and gazed at it and the
people on it.

Mr Noah said to Mrs Noah, "This one looks sensible. She hasn't picked us up and dropped us. She looks as if she might really care."

"I think she's gone to look at something else," said Mrs Noah. "We aren't new enough these days. We're not even clockwork, never mind batteries."

But Imogen had only gone to the shopkeeper, to ask if she might perhaps take the lid off and see what the inside was like.

"I try to keep it tidy," said Mrs Noah.

"You can't get the parts these days," Mr Noah was saying, looking at the broken windows.

Shem, their son, was remembering that he had often thought of mending the roof, but they had only brought two nails on board, like everything else, and they were not enough.

Grandpa was saying, "Imogen, it's time we went," and Imogen was having to tell him some important things. He was a good grandpa, and he listened. Then he was helping the shopkeeper lift the Ark down from its shelf to the floor.

The Ark was too old-fashioned for children these days, the shopkeeper said. His children played with it long ago and modernised it, and his grandchildren looked at it once and forgot it immediately.

"No," said Imogen, "it is not old-fashioned."

The shopkeeper was telling Grandpa that he thought he might have to start selling cyberpets, and it wouldn't feel like a toyshop any more.

Imogen did not listen to that. She sat on the shop floor and carefully lifted the wobbly red roof off. Inside were the rooms that Mr and Mrs Noah lived in,

with a rug on the floor, pots and pans
on the wall, and even a red telephone
on a shelf, which didn't really belong,
but was part of the modernisation. One
of Mr Noah's three sons sat at a table
drinking tea. Imogen did not know
which one he was.

The shopkeeper lifted up the whole deck, and all the other animals were inside in their little cabins, with places for hay and straw and tubs of water.

"Two of the sons are missing," he said. "They went to seek their fortune I expect. A giraffe has gone too. But everyone else is here."

"I think I will buy it," said Imogen, putting the deck down again in its place, and the damaged roof on the house part. "But Grandpa will have to pay. It won't be much, because it isn't new."

Grandpa said he would talk to the shopkeeper, and they went to the other side of the shop and had a conversation.

Imogen lifted the roof again, and put Mr and Mrs Noah inside, with the two lions. "If you don't mind them in your parlour," she said.

"They can sleep on the chairs," said Mrs Noah.

"That's what I thought," said Imogen. "But they might fall off when we carry you home."

"It will be an adventure," said Mr Noah.

Imogen had a piece of paper in her pocket, the sort with a sticky edge to keep it from blowing away. She borrowed the shopkeeper's pen, and wrote, "This probably belongs to Imogen", and stuck the note inside the Ark under the roof. She put the pen back on the shopkeeper's table.

"It'll be all right," she said to Mr Noah. "I think it has all been arranged.

Grandpa said, "I think we agree on that", and handed over some money. The shopkeeper wrote a receipt, with the pen Imogen had used, and gave it to Grandpa. Grandpa gave it to Imogen. "It's your Ark," he said, "and this receipt proves it."

Imogen said she would carry one end. Grandpa said he would use the wheelbarrow, tomorrow morning, because the shop was closing now, and Granny would have tea ready for them. "The Ark will be safe here," he said. "We shall come for it early. And you have the receipt, so it's yours."

"Goodnight, Mr Noah," said Imogen.

"I'll feed the animals," said Mr Noah.

"I'll get some milk for the lions," said Mrs Noah.

# TWO

Imogen went home and it was teatime. After that Granny telephoned Mummy and Daddy on the white telephone and had a conversation. Imogen had a conversation with Mummy, too. Mummy had a longer one with Imogen, but Imogen read a book at the same time, because the book had pictures.

Before going to sleep, she took the receipt from her pocket.

"What is that piece of paper?" asked Granny.

Imogen had to think for a moment what it was called. "It's a recipe," she said. "For the Ark."

"Keep it safe," said Granny.

Imogen looked at it, to see that the writing was still there. Some of it was joined up, so she could not read it, but there was the name of the shop in black print, and a number in red. I expect I don't understand it all, Imogen decided.

Then she understood about the number in red. It must be the telephone number of the Ark, because the Ark had a red telephone. 4 and 3 and 7.

"I can ring him up," she called to Granny.

"Time to go to sleep," said Granny.

If I had a telephone, Imogen thought, I would press the buttons, 4, and 3, and 7. She got comfortable on her pillow and pressed them.

Mr Noah was working with his son Shem, feeding the animals, giving them water, cleaning out the stables and pens and hutches, stroking the snakes, tickling the spiders, shining the elephants, putting the two lions back in their cage, talking to the monkeys so that one day they would say something sensible, and counting the mice.

"One, two," said Shem. "They won't keep still, but I think that's all."

"Two of everything," said Mr Noah. "The Ark is tidy and clean, and the animals all sleepy. We'll go upstairs and have our tea. It's an important day tomorrow."

"Don't tell the animals," said Shem. "They'll only get excited."

"We won't let the bats out tonight," said Mr Noah.

Upstairs, Mrs Noah was getting the pie out of the oven. It was a very good pie, with a painted crust, and they always enjoyed it every night.

Mrs Noah nearly dropped it when the red telephone rang its bell.

"Careful, Mother," said Shem.

"It hasn't done that before," said Mr Noah. "Don't touch it."

"It's an oven-timer," said Shem.

"I know when things are cooked without that," said Mrs Noah. "Let's eat our pie."

The telephone stopped ringing. Imogen had fallen asleep.

Afterwards Mr and Mrs Noah and Shem went out on the deck to see what the weather was like. It had been the same weather for a long time, all ceiling overhead, and walls to the east and west and north and south, and very calm.

"I wonder what it's like beyond all that," said Mrs Noah. "Out there."

"We shall never know," said Mr Noah.

"They've forgotten the stars again,"

said Mrs Noah. She remembered that there used to be stars at night, and sometimes a pretty moon, long ago.

"There used to be water," said Mr Noah. "It rained such a long time the whole world was water. We called it the Flood, and it ended with a rainbow."

Tonight there was a change. There were stars floating about the sky. Some of them fell down and played on the shop floor.

"Isn't that the moon?" said Mrs Noah. There was blue light coming into the shop, through the big front window.

Shem wondered whether it was the rainbow beginning again. When the last one happened he had been too young to see it.

"It's not the rainbow, like the old days," said Mr Noah. "Shall we bring the animals up to see it?"

"Is the pie scorching?" said Mrs

Noah. "I can smell smoke. Was that red thing a smoke alarm?"

Shem had been thinking about stars, and lights, and smoke. He said, "Father, Mother, I know what is happening. Those are not stars, that is not the rainbow, and there is no moon."

"Then what is it?" asked Mrs Noah.

"I don't know," said Shem. "It hasn't been like this before."

"Good," said Mrs Noah. "I don't like change."

It began to rain again. "We'd better go inside," said Mr Noah. "We know about rain."

Imogen woke up in the night. She had to tell Granny about a telephone call from the Ark, where Shem was telling his parents what was really happening.

"Don't kick," said Granny, when Imogen climbed in. "Your feet are cold.

What are you going to tell me?"

"I don't know," said Imogen, because she had quite forgotten on the way from her own bed. "I think it's raining."

"Go to sleep," said Granny. "It isn't getting into the house."

In the morning Grandpa insisted on having breakfast, when it was really time to go shopping. Imogen brought the piece of paper to remind him.

"It's the recipe," she explained, in case he had forgotten. "The toyshop, the Ark."

"I'll just read the paper a bit," said Grandpa. "To remind me what it's like outside."

Imogen was too busy to have breakfast.

After that Grandpa was a long time getting the wheelbarrow out of the garden shed, even though Imogen was helping him.

"It's all going wrong," said Imogen. "And Mr Noah is waiting."

"It's all going right," said Grandpa, putting Imogen in the barrow. She had not thought of that, so she was pleased. But she had to jump out again.

"Now what," said Grandpa.

"The recipe," said Imogen, running in for the piece of paper. "The telephone number."

At last they were out of the gate and going along the street. Sometimes the pavement was so narrow they had to use the road. The road had too many cars in it, not moving at all, so that it was difficult to get past. Then they couldn't go any further. There was no room for the wheelbarrow between the cars.

"The road's closed," said a policeman. "Big fire in the town during the night."

"We're just going to the toyshop," said Grandpa.

"To get my Ark," said Imogen.

"Look down the street," said the policeman. "You'll see where the fire was."

Grandpa looked. "Oh," he said.
"This isn't good news, Imogen." He
lifted her up, and she looked along the
street.

There was a fire engine. There was
smoke. There was a burnt shop like a
ruin. It was the toyshop, with daylight
coming through its windows.

"The Ark will be there," said
Imogen. "I've got the recipe. It belongs
to me."

"There were no toys left," said the
policeman. "I looked. Everything was
burnt."

Imogen knew what to do in an
emergency. Mrs Noah had thought she
looked sensible, and she was. "I haven't
had any breakfast," she said. "We'll go to
the teashop and have some."

Grandpa thought that Granny
would not mind. He parked the
wheelbarrow at a meter, and Imogen

had hot chocolate and an iced bun.

She wondered what Mr Noah was doing, and Grandpa mopped a tear from the end of her nose. You mostly have to be sensible when things go wrong. It doesn't put them right, but it's better than nothing.

# THREE

The night before, Mr Noah had sat in the doorway of the Ark's kitchen and watched the weather outside. There were clouds in the sky, under the ceiling. There were stars up there, and stars down below.

"I haven't seen one like this for a long time," he said. "Not since the old days, when the Ark sailed across the Flood. First the rain came down."

The rain was coming down now.

"It rattles on the roof," said Mrs Noah. "It's coming down the chimney. It'll get in the oven and spoil the pie."

Mr Noah put his hand outside, and it got water on it. "It's rain," he said. "I'd know it anywhere."

Shem had forgotten about rain. He was very young when the Ark first sailed, and it hadn't rained since.

"Don't go outside," said Mr Noah. "You get covered in water. It's called getting wet."

Shem went outside. He got very wet. "Oh Father," he said, "you do know a lot of things. But," he went on, "you don't know what's happening now."

"It's a storm," said Mr Noah. "God called it a tempest, and he's sent us another one. I was thinking we'd been forgotten. It's nice to be remembered."

He went on sitting in the doorway, watching the storm. "I'd nearly forgotten rain," he said.

"Lightning," he said, when there was a sudden flash of brightness. "It all comes back to me."

"Thunder," he said, when there was a great noise.

"No it isn't," said Shem.

"He's forgotten," said Mrs Noah. "There was your father, and me, and three little babies and the animals, and a storm. It was lovely, and we were all terrified. The rhinoceros was crying, poor dear. They're so sensitive."

"It isn't a storm," said Shem.

"Could be a volcano," said Mr Noah. "We're getting near the mountains, that's what. We're supposed to land on the mountains."

"It isn't a volcano," said Shem.

A huge raindrop came down, jumped in at the door, and sat on Mr Noah's lap, all cold and unsnuggly. Mr Noah stood up, dropped the rain on the floor, and closed the door.

"We'll stay dry inside," he said. "But we'd better go and look at the animals, and tell them what's going on."

Shem was trying to say that the shop was on fire, but he did not have the idea of houses or shops or fire, so it was hard to make himself clear. He scratched the backs of two fat black pigs instead.

That was just when Imogen was climbing into Granny's bed with her cold feet, and forgetting what she was thinking. I could ring up and ask them, she thought. I know it's them.

"What?" said Granny.

But Imogen had gone to sleep.

In the toyshop the thunder went on. Thunder sometimes sounds like pieces of house falling off. Sometimes it *is* pieces of house falling off.

"It's the sky getting loose," said Mrs Noah to herself, because Mr Noah and Shem were down below settling the animals. "I think that's a storm."

Round the Ark the sky of ceiling was tumbling to the floor. Over the Ark the water from the hosepipes of the fire brigade was falling worse than rain.

"I'm sure we'll get looked after,"
said Mrs Noah. "I'll put the kettle on in
case God comes visiting."

She could
hear noises like
giant footsteps
outside the Ark.
She was too
polite to look,
but if she had

she would have seen a chimney falling
down and going through the floor.

No one knocked at the door of the
Ark. Mrs Noah poured three mugs of
tea, and stood them in a neat row on
the table.

The first mug of tea wobbled a bit.
The tea twinkled, and the spoon fell out.

The second mug skipped a little bit,
and the tea jumped out.

The third one rolled right off the
table.

Mrs Noah sat down quite hard. The Ark had shaken itself, suddenly and wildly. "Mr Noah," called Mrs Noah. "Something is wrong, I think."

Mr Noah came up from below. He was soothing some snails, who had fallen from their shells and felt cold. "Now, now," he said, "Mrs Noah, don't say you have forgotten. We have done this before."

"Everything is swaying up and down," said Mrs Noah. "Where is my little boy?"

"He's a big boy now," said Mr Noah. "Mrs Noah, we are doing what the Ark was built for. We are sailing again. The rain has fallen deep enough to float us off, and we are sailing again, sailing, sailing."

"I want to stay here," said Mrs Noah. "That sensible child was going to look after us. Why isn't she here?"

"Sailing, sailing," said Mr Noah. "She was coming for us in the morning. Now all we have to do is sail to her. I'm sure that will save a lot of trouble."

"And where is Shem?" asked Mrs Noah.

"He is helping the animals say their prayers," said Mr Noah. "They wanted to do that, when the floor began to shake. Now, take care of these snails, and I shall go outside and steer. I think I remember how to do that. Send Shem up to look out from the front of the Ark, so that we don't hit a rock."

"And then what shall I do?" asked Mrs Noah.

"The rhinoceros is feeling funny again," said Mr Noah. "Go down and look after him."

Outside there was no sky ceiling, but real sky and real stars, and a whole shop full of water. The Ark was moving about gently, and did not know where to go. Mr Noah looked for a place to tie up until daylight, because sailing at night was so difficult. Once there had been forty days and forty nights of sailing, and the nights had been the worst.

The Ark went round and round in the middle of the water. The shop floor had fallen in when the chimney landed on it, and below it there was a cellar full of swirling water, and a sinky smell.

The Ark went down through the hole, past all the broken planks, into the blackness. The water whirled round and round, and everything was darker and darker. It was worse than any forty nights. The Ark was under the ground, in a tunnel, being washed away down a drain.

Then, all at once, there was bright daylight, and the Ark was in the air, falling, falling, out of the drain and towards the river.

Every animal shouted out. Mrs Noah worried about them all. "Mr Noah," she called, "what are you doing?"

"I'm in charge," said Mr Noah, remembering what to do. "I'll steer." And he steered the Ark the right way up into the jumpy river water.

Down below, the peacock felt ill and began to fade. He called out, but peacocks always sound ill, so Mrs Noah took no notice.

"Sailing, sailing," said Mr Noah. "Sailing."

# FOUR

Shem came on deck, very excited. "Father," he said, "we are afloat again. I was very little the first time it happened, and it is even better now I am bigger." Then the deck hiccuped under him, and he fell down into the hay and the monkeys laughed.

"Shem, just pat the elephants," said Mrs Noah. "They're feeling funny in their trunks. I'm going into the cabin to get your father a mug of tea."

Mr Noah was looking about the river. On one side of it fishing boats were tied up. On the other there was a high wall, with people walking behind it. Mr Noah very kindly called up to them, "Get into your boats. The water is going to cover the whole world. Get your families and your pets and sail with us."

No one took any notice of him. The people that saw him thought the Ark was an old log floating in the water, a broken tree in the river.

On the road, behind the wall, Imogen and Grandpa were standing for a moment, looking at the river.

"I'm very sorry about the Ark," said Grandpa. "I hope it doesn't spoil your stay with me and Granny. A sticky bun and a cup of hot chocolate are not a very fair exchange."

"I would have liked both," said Imogen. "But I have Mr Noah's telephone number, so I can keep in touch. It was on the recipe."

"So it is," said Grandpa, when Imogen showed him the receipt. "What is he doing now?"

"Grandpa," said Imogen, "you think he's been burnt up, but he hasn't. He's safe in the Ark. But I'll just make sure."

She knew the number, 437, even without looking. She leaned on the wall and looked at the river. She dialled the telephone of her mind.

Grandpa wanted to say something, but Imogen had to attend to the telephone.

"It's Mrs Noah," she said. "Can you hear, Grandpa?"

Mrs Noah did not understand the telephone. She heard it ring. She was going to take it to Mr Noah to get him to make it quiet, but it was fixed to the wall by a wire.

"How silly," she said. She called to Mr Noah, "It's making a noise again, Mr Noah. Come and stop it."

"They're getting him," said Imogen. "Grandpa, be quiet."

Mr Noah came into the cabin. "Ah, tea," he said. "Thank you, my dear." Then he listened to the telephone. "It's talking," he said. "Shem, will you check the mice, please. It sounds as if one of them has got out."

"Mr Noah," said Imogen.

"I'm too busy sailing to see to it," said Mr Noah. He was talking to Shem, but Imogen understood perfectly well, because busy is busy. Or, of course, you might not want to talk.

"Goodbye, then," said Imogen. She did not see Mr Noah coming out of the cabin with his tea. She did not see him seeing her and waving. She did not hear him shouting that he would be sailing back after the Flood was over, or telling her to build an Ark for herself. She did not even think the Ark was a log, because she did not see it at all.

Imogen went back to Granny and told her about the toyshop being burnt down, and Mr Noah being too busy to talk. Granny said, "Oh dear," but Imogen said it was all right, because she had the recipe.

The next day she went home, taking the receipt with her, and often meant to telephone Mr Noah.

When she had gone, Grandpa said to Granny, "I saw the remains of the Ark floating on the river, like an old log covered with ashes. Imogen was very brave."

Down on the river, away from the town, Mrs Noah was thinking, Mr Noah is very brave. Here we are going into the unknown world, and he knows what to do and so do Shem and the animals and I don't have to worry.

Mr Noah was thinking, I'd better not say, but I don't know what is to become of us. I won't tell Mrs Noah or Shem, or any of the animals, but there are dangers and I don't know what they are.

The river changed to being the sea. There were waves, and seagulls, and Mr Noah could see too far, because the edge of the sea was a long way off.

Just a flood, Mr Noah thought. It will dry up. That's the rule.

At home Imogen was reading about looking after rabbits, and where they could play. She telephoned Mr Noah to tell him that they needed a run to play in, and quite a lot of hay.

"Of course," said Mr Noah. "I won't forget."

So he knew what to do the next day, when the Ark saw a piece of land, and found its way to it, and then sat on it.

"Have we got home?" Mrs Noah

45

asked, looking over the side. "The ground is yellow, with waves in it."

"It is the desert," said Mr Noah. "We have landed at last, after a short flood. The animals can all go out and have a run. They can have a picnic and sleep on the sand for a change."

The animals went out, two by two, just as they had come aboard. They walked about on the sand and left footprints. They had never seen footprints before, and all the little ones thought something was chasing them.

They had their picnic, and played.

"It was a good idea, Mr Noah," said Mrs Noah.

"It just came to me," said Mr Noah. "Like a message." He lit a fire in the desert. There was a lot of firewood in the sand.

Night was coming. Animals settled down to sleep on the sand, glad the voyage was over. Mrs Noah was glad too. Shem was wondering whether they couldn't have a different pie one day. Mr Noah was glad not to be sailing in the dark. The fire sang to itself, and sparks went up.

The night was warm and peaceful. But all at once there was a fuss beginning among the tigery people.

Shem said "Hush, I'll open the tin of tiger food."

The tigery people were not hungry. They were wet. Water was creeping up over the desert, running in and out, in and out, a little higher each time. It woke the animals, two by two. It tickled Mrs Noah's feet, and woke her up. It trod on the fire and put it out.

"But it hasn't been raining," said Mr Noah, going out with his Ark light to look. He did not know that the tide went out each day and came in again, because he was only used to flood. The animals had been sleeping on a beach, not on a dry desert, and the tide was coming in, ripple by ripple.

It was a scramble to get the animals aboard. Shem drove them to the gangplank, Mr Noah sent them to their pens or stables or cages, and Mrs Noah dried their feet, or sometimes whole small soaked animals.

Shem climbed aboard just as the waves came right round the Ark and made it tip up at one end.

"We shall be drowned," said Mr Noah. "It will go right over us. This is the worst flood I ever knew."

But a moment later the Ark lifted at the other end as well. Animals fell over and shouted. The Ark bounced, rose to the top of the water, and floated again.

Mrs Noah put on the kettle for a pot of tea. The animals had extra hay and lumps of sugar.

# FIVE

In the morning the land was a long way off. Mrs Noah said, "It's just a flood, Mr Noah."

Mr Noah said, "If I'm with you, Mrs Noah, I can live through all these little problems. It would be nice to have Ham and Japheth back."

"I often wonder what those naughty boys are doing." said Mrs Noah.

"And that poor spotty animal is lonely too," said Shem, "now that there's only one of it."

"And there's nothing we can do to help it," said Mr Noah. "It's one thing to  take imaginary animals on board, but I don't believe in that spotty one at all."

A long way off Imogen was at school colouring in a picture. "Not really spots," she was saying, "but patches of colour. I am making a green giraffe," she told her teacher.

 "That's why we never see them among the trees," said the teacher. He knew his natural history.

The Ark seemed to stay still all day, and the land got further away. Mr Noah felt that was right, because the Ark had all the animals on board, and the land would come back for them when it was ready.

After lunch there was smoke far away. Mrs Noah went round with a broom and duster. Shem brushed the animals. Mr Noah looked at his maps.

"It's a burning mountain," he said. "Or God is coming to inspect us. Be ready for both."

He was quite wrong. At teatime a big ship came by, with smoke pouring from its funnel. It gave a great shout like a sea monster, and went on its way through the dusk. There was a bright green light to one side, and a red one to the other.

"We should have lights," said Mr Noah. "We are a ship too."

"But," said Mrs Noah, "we don't want to be seen. We must go quietly on our way, not bothering anybody, not being bothered by them. If God wants us he can find us."

"Yes," said Mr Noah. "You are right. I wish he would find our other boys, Ham and Japheth, and bring them back."

They had their tea, and spent a quiet night. Mr Noah and Shem looked at the stars, learning them one by one, specially the flying ones. "They might be angels," Mr Noah told Shem. "Remember them."

"I think I can hear them singing," said Shem.

He was wrong about the stars singing. In the morning the Ark was not the only thing floating on the face of the waters. There were five fishing boats in a circle round the Ark, and the fishermen were singing as they threw their nets out.

Down below in the Ark the animals tried to learn the songs. They were not very good at it. Mrs Noah went to give them medicine, because she was sure they had pains in the tummy.

Mr Noah thought of songs he used to know. He sat by the fire and hummed them to himself, and was very sleepy. He dreamed that the fishermen's songs had become very loud and ugly. Shem woke him to say that the fishermen had caught their fish, and the seagulls had come down to help.

Mr Noah looked. "See that our birds do not escape and join them," he said. "We must not lose any more from our list."

Shem went to make sure of that. He came back to tell Mr Noah there was nothing to worry about, but that the animals were now singing seagull songs, which were not very pretty.

"Good," said Mr Noah, watching the fishing boats, and seeing the nets being pulled up on board. "It is very kind of the fishermen to take so many fish on board and keep them safe. We have only got land animals, and birds, and have no room for fish. I am glad someone is caring for them." He thought he must be right about that. "I'm sorry for the fish that are thrown back, because that means they are not going to live when the flood dries up."

Things began to happen that Mr Noah was not at all prepared for. Something bumped into one side of the Ark. Then another thing banged into the other side. At the back an ugly coil of fishing net began to take hold. The net was all round the Ark and pulling it towards a fishing boat.

Like the fish the men were catching, the Ark had been caught, and was being lifted up, and would soon be tipped out into the bottom of the fishing boat.

"But we have already been saved," Mr Noah shouted. "We are already doing God's work. There is no need to look after us."

At that moment, far away, Imogen thought of Mr Noah and the Ark, of Mrs Noah and the animals. Well, she thought, I am really meant to be getting the school scissors and cutting this piece of string to be a bird's leg with the claw hanging down. So she went to do that.

"Mrs Noah," called Mr Noah, "get your scissors and cut the net. Shem, get your large knife." Mr Noah got the big axe, and chopped at the net, because that was tough brown string.

They were busy chopping and

slicing and snipping, and Imogen was cutting her string. "I have done it specially well," she said.

"It certainly looks like string," said the teacher, kindly. "Now put a foot on it and make it a bird's leg."

Mr Noah was saying, "It certainly looks like string, but much tougher." Chop, went the axe, and chop, and the strands of string parted. The net slipped away from the Ark, and it began to float away from the fishing boats. It had got very near to them, and the noise of the seagulls was very loud.

Fishermen shouted to each other to look out for that old lump of wood, and began to push the Ark away with their boat's oars.

"Mind our paint," Mr Noah called.

"Be off with you," the fishermen called.

Mr Noah chopped at another length of net. It let go of the Ark, and the Ark floated free once more.

"We have escaped again," said Mr Noah. "I hope we have another quiet night after all that."

It was not quiet yet, because of the screaming seagulls, and the animals below trying to join in their songs and the fishermen's chants.

"We'll go and calm them down," said Mr Noah. "Mrs Noah, don't you think it is time for tea?"

"I shall put the kettle on," said Mrs Noah. "When I have swept the bits of string from the deck."

Imogen put the legs and feet on her bird, and finished it. She began to make another. Two by two, she thought; I shall be in charge of the Ark.

At the Ark, Mrs Noah went round the deck throwing bits of net back into the sea. A seagull came to look. It decided not to eat string, but picked Mrs Noah up instead, because she was bigger, and flew off with her, laughing a lot.

Mrs Noah shouted as loud as she could for Mr Noah. By the time he heard her, the seagull had found she was only made of wood and dropped her a long way off.

Mrs Noah should have fallen straight into the sea, but other seagulls caught her on the way down, one after the other, chewed her cruelly round the middle, screamed at her, and then dropped her into the sea.

There she floated, face down. Mr Noah shouted for her. She heard him. But she could only call back in little bubbles, and no one heard her.

# SIX

At school, far away, Imogen was not putting two and two together by making paper birds, but adding hard numbers like five and eight. Then, instead of doing that stuff she sat and looked out of the window and wondered about other numbers like 4 and 3 and 7, and telephoning the Ark. She was sure she ought to.

Her teacher asked whether five and eight were bothering her, because if they were he would tell her more about them.

Imogen said that five and eight were not numbers bothering her. It just worried her that no one was answering 437, so she knew something was wrong. But she could not talk about telephones and the Ark at school, because they were not part of lessons.

Mr Noah had heard Mrs Noah calling for him. He did not understand what had happened to her. Nothing had ever happened to her before, and she had always been there to hear him, answer him, and get the pie out of the oven.

"Perhaps she has gone shopping," he said, when he had searched the deck and the cabin, and Shem had asked the animals whether she was down in the hold with them.

"But I heard her in the sky," said

Mr Noah. "She is a very sensible person. Why has she gone away?" He asked a seagull whether he knew anything about Mrs Noah.

"She fell in the sea," said the seagull. "Over there. She was made of wood, you know."

"Can you get her back for us?" asked Mr Noah.

"We only catch fish," said the seagull. "Not wooden ladies." He gave one of his big screams and flew away.

Shem tied a rope round his middle. Mr Noah held the end of it, and Shem went into the sea to find his mother. But the rope was not very long, and the sea was so big, and all he found was a crab.

At last Mr Noah hauled him in, and Shem sat shivering on the deck, cold and wet and unhappy.

"God is angry with us," said Mr Noah. "That is the problem, and we can do nothing about it."

"And that bell has been ringing in the cabin," said Shem. But it had stopped now, because Imogen was thinking of other numbers like thirteen.

It grew dark, and Mr Noah and Shem fed the animals. The animals really wanted Mrs Noah, because some of them felt ill when the Ark rocked about, and did not want their suppers. Mr Noah and Shem stood on the deck. Mr Noah shouted, "Mrs Noah, my love, come back to us," and Shem called, "Mother, Mother, we can't do without you." But there was no reply.

"She is made of wood," said Shem. "She will float."

"Her paint will wash off," said Mr Noah. "We shall not recognise her."

"We shall know her voice," said Shem. "And the pie she will cook."

"Her eyes will run," said Mr Noah. "She will not recognise us."

That night they had the pie, as usual. "I am not very hungry," said Mr Noah. "I will go down to the animals and talk to them, because they are very restless."

"The Flood is getting rough," said Shem. "It makes them feel strange."

The hippopotamus, the otter, the seal, and Mr and Mrs Whale, wanted to look for Mrs Noah. It was kind of them, Mr Noah said, but they must stay in the Ark, because God had told Noah to keep them there until the Flood went down. "We have done wrong already," he said. "We must not do so again." He left them to sleep. They would feel more comfortable, he said.

The waves grew rougher. Wind howled in the chimney, and smoke came down into the cabin. The teapot went slip-slop, and the kettle rattled its lid.

Far away on the land, Imogen was in the bath, sliding about and making waves. The waves jumped over the ends of the bath. "That's wrong," said her mother, but Imogen knew it was right. She was taken out of the warm water and dried and put to bed. She thought she was like a new pink hippopotamus, in her stable in the Ark.

Out at sea, Mr Noah had a sleep while Shem steered the Ark through the Flood. He tried to steer it to his mother, but no one knew where she was. She will climb on board, Shem thought, and he stared into the fierce wind until his eyes were cold. But no matter how much he looked, the night was dark, with not even a single star.

Mr Noah woke up from an unhappy dream, and came to take his turn at steering. He did not know where to go, either. He did not look into the wind, but listened. He thought he would hear Mrs Noah come close and shout. Then he would put out a strong hand to lift her on board. But it did not happen. It did not happen so many times that Mr Noah's tears ran down his cheeks and splashed into the Flood.

Shem came to see his father.
"I have been washed out of my bed,"

he said. "A wave untucked me and dropped me on the floor, so I thought it might be drier and warmer out here. Where are we sailing, Father?"

"To a mountain," said Mr Noah. "That is where we should land."

"I do not think God cares any more," said Shem.

"We wouldn't be having bad times if God did not want us to have better ones later," said Mr Noah. "We must go on sailing to the mountain, and everything will come right."

Then a wave came right over the Ark, and threw Mr Noah under the rail, and Shem on the roof. There was so much shouting from the hold that Mr Noah thought the animals had fallen out and would float away.

Shem said, "It is light enough to see the moon."

"And bright enough to see the

stars," said Mr Noah. "Except to the south, down there, where it is still night."

"We are going back into the night," said Shem. "Sail the other way, Father, into the sunshine."

Noah steered towards where the clouds were turning white and the bright sky glowing blue. But, though he steered as hard as he could, the Flood was going a different way. The Ark was going back towards the night.

"I do not care what happens," said Mr Noah. "My Mrs Noah has been taken from me, and I have failed to keep the animals safe. I think that is the last blue sky I shall ever see. I shall never reach it."

Shem was shouting, "Go towards the light, Father, towards the light."

"Tomorrow," said Mr Noah. "Today is just another night. Tomorrow God will be pleased. Today he is not. We shall not enjoy it, but no harm will come to us. We must sit still and bear our troubles."

"Father," Shem shouted. He had to shout over the noise of the wind. "That is not night. Those are rocks."

"Mountains," said Mr Noah. "After all that, in the worst moment, when we have lost Mrs Noah, and everything seemed hopeless, we have reached the end of our journey."

"No, no," called Shem. "There are rocks. The Ark is going to hit the rocks. It is not the end of the journey God sent us on, but a shipwreck."

"Don't be silly and excited," said Mr Noah. "The shipwreck happened to other people. We land gently on a mountain, and it has been written down. That is what we shall do. But that, Shem, is only a dark cloud. It will last all night, but in the morning the sky will be blue, and one day we shall see the mountain."

He looked, and he looked, but the wrong way. He would have been right if the dark shadow had been the night. But Shem was right. The Ark sailed backwards on to the rocks, Mr Noah sat hard on the deck, and the cabin fell down all round him.

# SEVEN

At school Imogen began to tidy her table. The others had not finished making their boxes, so she was first. She put the box to one side, and gathered up all the card and paper and put it in the bin. She put the top on the paste and took it to the cupboard. She went back to her place and sat down.

It would have been better not to put the newly made box on the chair.

Then she would not have sat on it.

No one else had noticed. Imogen went to the cupboard, got the pot of paste, and started again.

Down by the sea another storm wave got behind the Ark and lifted it away from the rocks. Mr Noah looked at the tumbled cabin. "There's nothing to worry about there," he said. He had built the Ark with his own hands, so he knew he could put matters right. "I might even make some improvements," he said. "What a silly boy Shem is sometimes. We just hit a hard bit of night, the sleepiest bit. In the morning I shall get my hammer and put the cabin right. I like that sort of work."

He was happier with something to do. Steering is all very well, but if you don't know where you are going and it is night time, then it is not much fun. "But I don't expect it to be," said Mr

Noah. "Now, Shem, come down from the roof and we'll see to the anima . . ."

But he did not finish what he had to say, because another wave came along, picked up the whole Ark, lifted it high in the air, and dropped it on the land, on a wet black rock. The wave went out to sea and left the Ark where it was. The wave's friends came to see what it had done, and jumped about making foam and splashing in an inconsiderate way, shouting and crashing and gurgling.

The Ark lay split and broken, its cabin crushed, on the wet black rock. The animals were silent for a long time, thinking they must have been drowned or squashed. But gradually an elephant's trunk felt its way about, a mouse or two twitched a whisker and peered from its hole, a tigery person wanted to talk about breakfast, and both rhinoceroses

said that things were better now that the
people in the next cage were not
rocking the boat; and the hedgehogs
said it was not them.

"I wonder whether a hammer will be enough," Mr Noah said, looking at all the damage. "I wish your mother was here, Shem. She would help me make up my mind."

"I've made mine up," said Shem. "We can't mend that, Father. We'll have to leave it, set the animals free, and go back to being farmers."

"Yes," said Mr Noah. "I remember being a farmer. We'll have to go and find a field." But he really thought they should have landed peacefully on a mountain.

"We didn't," said Shem. "I don't know where you got that idea, Father."

"There should be a rainbow," said Mr Noah. "I've read the book. I probably wrote that bit. It's just come out different now that we're actually doing it."

"I should go and look for Mother," said Shem. "She would expect that. You

stay here, Father, and mend the Ark, and
we can live in that. First we must find a
cave for the animals, and then we shall
see what is in store for us."

"If only," said Mr Noah, "that girl
had come back for us before the
thunderstorm when the Ark sailed again.
We would have been on dry land, and
quite safe."

"It was the world on fire," said
Shem. "The wooden sky, and the
horizon, and burning stars."

"I won't argue with you," said Mr
Noah. "Let us look at the animals, then
find the cave you were talking about."

Shem climbed up into the Ark,
and into the hold. Mr Noah went
through the cabin. He rescued the
pie, and tidied up.

Just then Imogen's telephone
tinkled twice. When she lifted it up
there was only a noise like the sea far

away. "They are safe," said Imogen, and her mother said, "What are you talking about?"

The animals were being as comfortable as they could. There was salt in their hay, they said. It was nice for a change, but not for every meal.

"We shall find you a dry cave," said Mr Noah.

"We are going to find it now," said Shem.

Higher up the land there was a dry cave. "God will provide," said Mr Noah. "The Flood has gone down and we shall live here."

There was a problem at once. Mr Noah had only just walked into the cave when two people came rushing up to him, shouting angrily.

"Stop," said the one with a beret on his head. "This is our cave already, is that not so, Marc."

"It is so, Gaston," said the other, with the small moustache. "We live here with our mother. There is no room for you. Please go away, ancient man."

"Then we shall go away," said Mr Noah. He thought that was a pity, because the cave was large and comfortable.

Shem came into the cave then. "This is Marc, and this is Gaston," said Mr Noah. "It is their cave, and they live here with their mother. We shall have to find another."

"Marc?" said Shem. "Gaston? Mother?"

"Oui," said Marc; and Gaston said, "C'est vrai."

And their mother said, "Shem? Shem, is that you? Mr Noah, where have you been all this time?"

And Mrs Noah came from the back of the cave, where she had been cooking. She had bite marks round her middle, from the seagull, but they had healed, and her eyes had dried.

"Gaston?" said Mr Noah. "You are my son Ham."

"Papa," said Ham, or Gaston. He had been away from home so long that he had forgotten the words of his own language.

"Daddy," said Marc, or Japheth, who had been quite little when he left.

"Mrs Noah," said Mr Noah, kissing her. "We have all been brought together again."

"I shall put on the kettle," said Mrs Noah, when she had kissed all of them and sat them by the fire.

Later on that day all the animals from the Ark walked two by two into the cave. "Except for that imaginary one," said Mr Noah. "She is one by one."

"The camelopard," said Ham, or Gaston. "We have had the other with us all these years. They will be glad to be together once more, n'est-ce pas?"

"Camelopard?" said Mr Noah. "That is an imaginary name for an imaginary animal."

"It is what they call it where we have been," said Ham. "The words are different. Gaston is the French for Ham, Marc is the French for Japheth, and camelopard is the French for giraffe."

The two animals were pleased
to see one another, but the lady
camelopard from the Ark sniffed, and
said, "My dear, you have been eating
garlic. Hay is so much better for you."

At home Imogen opened her book
to show the giraffe she had painted. She
had closed the book too soon, and now,
on the opposite page, there was a copy.
"Two by two," said Imogen. "Two
giraffes."

But in the Ark camelopards are imaginary, says Mr Noah.

Mr Noah took his hammer and his folding rule and went back to the Ark, to measure and mend.

"There's much work to be done," he said, when he came back to the cave. "We shall need everyone to help us repair it and put it back on the Flood. We shall need oxen and horses and elephants to move it back to the water. And then we shall all sail for the mountain, where we are supposed to land."

That night, by a fire of thistle stalks, Mr Noah's family, and all God's creatures, knelt and prayed for a fortunate voyage to come.

"I'm glad we did," said Mrs Noah long afterwards.

"Amen," said the whole family and the animals, then and long afterwards.

# EIGHT

M r Noah was right. There was much work to be done. The Ark hung on the edge of the rocks where the sea had thrown it. More sea came up and looked inside through cracks and splits. Wind rattled the roof. Rain scratched the paint. The sun made dark shadows.

"It is like building it again," said Mr Noah.

Ham, Shem, and Japheth gathered

tough grass stalks and Mrs Noah twisted
ropes out of them. Mr Noah first tied the
Ark to the rock to keep it from being
washed away. Then he and the three
sons cut down a huge bramble bush
and made rollers and levers, and turned
the Ark round to a safer position.

With the help of strong animals
they hauled it upright. Mr Noah rebuilt
the cabin, and made a new chimney
from a length of waterpipe.

Some animals were allowed outside to eat green leaves, but the grass cut their mouths and the other leaves were too strong. Mrs Noah found an apple and rolled it to the cave and baked it.

"I've been wanting a change from pie," said Shem.

"We longed for pie," said Gaston and Marc (they had got so used to these names). "With a painted top."

Imogen woke one morning and instantly dialled 437, to tell Mr Noah what was outside. She thought he would be glad to know about snow falling so pretty on every roof and burying every wall.

Mr Noah was digging with a shovel he had made from an elder stem, getting the cold and nasty snow out of the way so that he could mend the side of the Ark. Imogen ran about and threw snow at Daddy, and fed the garden birds. Shem and his brothers opened tins of lion food and shared out stacks of hay.

The days grew darker and the nights grew longer. Shem said the cave was running out of hay. Mrs Noah said that the snowflakes looked like the miracle food called manna; and when it was carefully served the animals liked it. Mrs Noah knew many useful old stories.

The snow went away and the nights grew shorter. One evening Mr Noah came home to the cave, very tired but pleased. "Everything is ready," he said. "The Flood is coming up higher, and in the morning we can all go on board and set out for the mountain."

That was a story he knew; but there are other stories also.

For now he was right. The animals walked on board, from large to small, lion with lion, elephant with elephant, camelopard with giraffe. And just at that very time of that very day Imogen arranged all her shoes and boots and slippers in twos and put them in a long

line across her bedroom. Granny was visiting at that time, and asked why she did it. Imogen said she did not know. But that morning she had thought of 4 and 3 and 7, and the next moment of all the animals walking into the Ark, and seen two giraffes.

"Come and have breakfast," said Granny.

Water rose under the Ark. One end lifted free. Mr Noah and all three sons waded out and cut the ropes at that end. The middle came free, and they cut the ropes there. They climbed on board, and when the back end floated they cut the ropes there. The Ark was on the Flood once more.

"We are saved," said Shem.

"Wait till we get to the mountain," said Mr Noah.

"Wait until we get anywhere," said Mrs Noah.

"Au revoir," Gaston and Marc shouted to the land.

"And throw that garlic overboard," said Mrs Noah.

Down below, a camelopard felt seasick.

The Ark sailed all day, and the day after that. The land went away. Mr Noah said that land doesn't move, and it must be the Flood getting deeper.

Later on, when everybody else was having a nap, Mr Noah thought he saw land again. He thought he saw a mountain, but it was not very clear; or something was wrong with it. Perhaps land does move about, he told himself. Or perhaps, he began to think, it isn't land. He called for Shem.

Shem looked and called for Gaston. Ham called for Marc, or Japheth. They didn't like the look of it, they said, don't tell Maman.

They meant they didn't like the way this land looked at them with its eye. They didn't like the way it turned round and looked at them with its other eye. It had one each side.

Between the eyes was a mouth. The mountain opened the mouth and swam towards them.

Mrs Noah came out on deck then.

"What a pretty cave," she said. "But why has it got teeth?"

"Sea monster," said Mr Noah. "It wasn't on the list God gave us. Don't worry."

"Zut," said Gaston. "Saperlipopette."

"Alors," said Marc. "Formidable."

The sea monster kept on swimming. One jaw went under the Ark, one jaw went on top. The monster swallowed a mouthful of sea and Ark, down and down, gurgling down into the darkness.

"That's not in our flood," said Mr
Noah. "We'd better all close our eyes
and say prayers about being rescued.
We're in the wrong book. This isn't our
story, but Jonah's."

Imogen was in her bed at midnight,
she thought. She woke up feeling
watery inside, and covered with
darkness. Granny was still there.
Granny said, "Close your eyes, then
it won't be so dark."

In the Ark the animals found it was
true, not quite so dark if you close your
eyes to keep it out.

"But we don't want it out of us,"
said Mr Noah. "We want us out of it.
What shall we do, when we have said
our prayers?"

The monster opened its mouth and
swallowed a huge lump of seaweed.
Daylight came in for a moment or two.
Then it swallowed the last floating rock

in the world, because no one has seen any since. Each time there was daylight.

"Where there is daylight," said Gaston, or Ham, "there is a way out, n'est-ce pas?"

"Parfois," said Marc, or Japheth.

"Next time," said Shem, "we shall sail out."

"If we have time," said Mr Noah. "But we may take too long and be crushed by those teeth."

"Ah ha," said Gaston.

"Voyez-vous," said Marc.

The sea monster got ready to swallow again. Mr Noah got ready to steer. Shem had a pole ready to push them clear. Gaston had his hands in his pockets, and Mrs Noah thought he was being lazy, and that it came from living away from the Ark for too long.

The monster bit an island covered with trees. Mr Noah steered extremely hard. Shem pushed against teeth, but the jaws were closing. The island went by, and down the throat, splash into its stomach.

Still Gaston did not help. He stood at the front end of the Ark and watched.

Still Marc did not help. He stood at the back of the Ark, with his hands in his pockets.

Then, at the last moment, when Shem had not managed to hold the monster's teeth apart, and the Ark was being swallowed down again, Gaston did something. It was not very much, and did not look helpful. He held out his hands on either side. He squeezed something between his hands, and scattered something from them over the side.

That was all he did.

At the other end of the Ark, Marc took something from his pocket and twisted it over the side.

At the taste of what Gaston had thrown, the monster's jaws opened again, and it drank the sea, as much as it could, like a tidal wave.

At the taste of what Marc had sprinkled, the monster coughed like a hurricane.

It spat out the Ark, and went on spitting out islands, coughing out floating rocks, and gargling stray ships.

There was a strong smell. There was something stinging in the air.

"I thought I told you–" Mrs Noah began to say. But Gaston knew what she meant.

"I shall wash my hands, Mother," he said. "Though I think they smell very tasty."

"You are a naughty son," said Mrs Noah. "I am glad to say."

He had crushed garlic into the

monster's mouth. The monster had not liked that, and opened his mouth. Marc had sprinkled pepper after pepper, and the monster had sneezed.

"I think I am going to be sick," said Imogen.

"Oh dear," said Granny, babysitting.

"Or I might just feel better," said Imogen.

# NINE

Everything felt safer after the monster. "And we have got rid of that garlic," said Mrs Noah. "Back to proper home cooking, Ham, Japheth. Shem has never wanted strange food."

They had pie that night, as usual. Mrs Noah knew what was best, and she knew that her household was right again, with everybody there.

Mr Noah was still looking for his

mountain. "I'll be glad to retire," he said, "and go back to farming, with one goat, one mule, and six hens, instead of two of a hundred kinds, not all friendly." He had had his paint scratched by a crocodile.

"Well, Father," said Ham, "it all depends on the steering, and you are best at that."

Mr Noah had been looking at the map, but all the land was off the edge, and there was nothing but Flood, which doesn't show up on a map. "A drawing would have been better," he said.

Imogen was drawing the sea at school, splashing about on the computer. She found that some of her birds were swimming, and some of her fish were flying, and there wasn't any land. Her drawing did not help Mr Noah, but at least she was thinking about him.

The telephone in the Ark was not working at all well, because Ham was being Gaston and had taken it to pieces and found nothing useful inside but a ringing bell.

Mr Noah was studying the water. He knew about floods, he said. "This one is getting deeper, I can tell. When it gets to the mountain it will reach the top, and then we shall have to wait for it to go down. That's all. That's why we can't see the mountain. It's down below."

"He's so clever, your father," said Mrs Noah. "He can explain anything."

The next morning there was land to be seen, and it was coming nearer. In the morning it was grey. At midday it was green with trees. In the afternoon there were houses. In the evening there were people walking about.

One of them was not Imogen.

Imogen was in bed, reading one of Granny's books, and wondering about going to sleep, but not yet.

"It's very odd," said Mr Noah, out on the river, thinking of staying awake, seeing everybody up there on the land. "We were supposed to be the last people in the world. I suppose God has changed his mind."

"Or we did not understand him," said Mrs Noah. "Are you sure you listened all the time, Mr Noah?"

"If it was about sailing," said Mr Noah, "I might not have understood. I am really only a farmer. I wonder if we shall land on a farm."

In the darkness of the night none of them knew where they were. Shem said the land was on his side of the Ark.

"No," said Ham, "it is on my side."

"It is at the front," said Japheth.

"You never did agree, you boys,"

said Mrs Noah. "Even when all three of you were right at the same time." Because all of them were right: there was land to the left, and the right, and ahead.

Only Mr Noah could tell that the sea was far behind them. The Ark was going up the river. "It's not the way to get up a mountain," he said. "We've been shipwrecked, we've been swallowed, and I dare say we are now going to be sunk."

The Ark came up the river to the houses, and to the wall beside the water, with all the fishing boats the far side of the river.

Mr Noah looked at the wall. "I think it is the end of the world," he said. "It has to stop somewhere, after all, so why not here?"

"But what is happening?" asked Mrs Noah.

"I dare say God has closed the book," said Mr Noah. "That's all."

But Imogen had only dropped Granny's book that she had been reading, and closed her eyes.

"Dropped it, gone to sleep," said Mr Noah.

"What shall we do?" said Mrs Noah.

"Keep on steering," said Mr Noah. "Perhaps a cup of tea would be helpful, and a slice of pie."

The river began to rush about, and

get higher. Mr Noah tried to steer away
from the stone wall. "I like the Flood," he
said, "but not the hard edges."

The sky grew dark. Mrs Noah
shrieked. Mr Noah held tight. The Ark
had come to the wall, but instead of
hitting it, it had gone into a gap among
the hard stones, into a midnight drain,
pushed there by the fast water, pushed
along in the dark, with no stars to help.

"Swallowed by the land," said Mr
Noah. "We have not got anywhere at all."

"I'm sure it will be all right, Mr
Noah," said Mrs Noah, coming along in
the dark with tea and pie. "I'm sure you
have done your best."

Imogen was doing her best too.
She was staying with Granny again.
She was thinking, that morning, of a
sticky bun and some hot chocolate.
She decided it would not make her sad
or remind her about the shop that burnt

down, or losing the Ark.

"Very well," said Grandpa. "We'll just have a good breakfast first, to get into practice."

Then they went down into the town. This time there was no policeman to turn them away. There was no burning toyshop.

"It's an antique shop now," said Grandpa. "Tables and chairs and cupboards."

"Not interesting," said Imogen. But just to check that Grandpa was right, she stopped by the new glass window and looked in. There were lots of tables, and sideboards, and grumpy pictures.

"Come on," said Grandpa. He wanted her to pass the bicycle shop and the pencil shop and the scrubbing-brush shop without doing any shopping, or even thinking about it. Even if she didn't buy anything she still had to make choices.

Imogen opened the door of the antique shop. She knew what she wanted. Grandpa said, "Imogen," but that did not delay her for an instant. He had to follow her in.

Imogen was talking to the shopkeeper. There was a new shopkeeper in this new shop. "We found it in the cellar this morning," he was saying. "It floated up the drain from the river. It isn't every day that I see a Noah's Ark like this, with Noah's family and all the animals  in it. I expect I shall sell it for a lot of money."

"No," said Imogen, "you can't sell it."

"But it's mine," said the shopkeeper.

Imogen was looking in her purse. The piece of paper was safely there. "This is the recipe," she said. "I bought it last year, in this shop. It has been round the world since, but it has come back to me. Also—"  and she lifted the roof of the Ark. She saw Mr Noah, Mrs Noah, and the three sons. She looked in the top of the roof, and there was her piece of paper with the sticky edge, still sticking, still saying, "This probably belongs to Imogen."

"And that's you?" said the man.

"Me," said Imogen.

"Then it must be yours," said the shopkeeper, giving back the receipt. "It wasn't here yesterday, so it must have sailed back on purpose for you."

"Of course," said Imogen.

"Of course," said Mrs Noah. "I said she was a sensible girl and would wait."

They didn't need a wheelbarrow. Grandpa and the shopkeeper carried the Ark between them back to Granny's house, and put it in Imogen's bedroom.

Imogen sat and gazed at the Ark all morning, and again all the evening. She forgot about her tea, about her dinner, about her sticky bun and hot chocolate at the teashop, which she had not had.

Mrs Noah offered her a slice of pie, which was better than all those things. One giraffe smelt of garlic for ever.

"You are clever," said Imogen. "Going round the world and coming back."

"We said our prayers," said Mrs Noah. "That was the reply."

"Amen," said Mr Noah.

"Sapristi," said Gaston, or Ham.

# About the author

William Mayne found it was easier to
write books than do his schoolwork,
and had his first one published in 1953.
By the millennium he will have had
about a hundred in print, but he still
works very slowly and spends whole
days looking out of the window not
doing the gardening and pretending he
is thinking. When it is dark he gets out
the ink and write words down until they
make sense. He knows that you don't
get much done if you are busy.